Spot the Shape

Shapes in Sport

Rebecca Rissman

Heinemann
LIBRARY

www.heinemann.co.uk/library

Visit our website to find out more information about Heinemann Library books.

To order:

☎ Phone 44 (0) 1865 888066

📄 Send a fax to 44 (0) 1865 314091

💻 Visit the Heinemann Bookshop at www.heinemann.co.uk/library to browse our catalogue and order online.

Heinemann Library is an imprint of Capstone Global Library Limited, a company incorporated in England and Wales having its registered office at 7 Pilgrim Street, London, EC4V 6LB – Registered company number: 6695582

"Heinemann" is a registered trademark of Pearson Education Limited, under licence to Capstone Global Library Limited

Text © Capstone Global Library Limited 2009
First published in hardback in 2009
The moral rights of the proprietor have been asserted.

Edited by Rebecca Rissman, Charlotte Guillain and Catherine Veitch
Designed by Joanna Hinton-Malivoire
Picture research by Tracy Cummins and Heather Mauldin
Originated by Dot Gradations Ltd
Printed in China by South China Printing Company Ltd

ISBN 978 0 431 19292 5 (hardback)
13 12 11 10 09
10 9 8 7 6 5 4 3 2 1

British Library Cataloguing in Publication Data

Rissman, Rebecca
Shapes in sport. - (Acorn. Spot the shape)
516.1'5
A full catalogue record for this book is available from the British Library.

Acknowledgements

We would like to thank the following for permission to reproduce photographs: ©Alamy pp. **4** (Barrie Rokeach), **11** (SBP), **12** (SBP); ©Getty Images pp. **7** (David Madison), **8** (David Madison), **13** (Debra McClinton), **14** (Debra McClinton), **15** (Dugald Bremner), **16** (Dugald Bremner), **17** (Doug Pensinger), **18** (David Madison), **19** (Stockbyte), **20** (Stockbyte), **23** (Dugald Bremner); ©Jupiter Images pp. **9** (Corbis), **10** (Corbis); ©Shutterstock pp. **6** (Saniphoto), **21** (Jonathan Larsen).

Cover photograph of a football on a field reproduced with permission of ©Superstock/Corbis. Back cover photograph of a bicycle reproduced with permission of ©Getty Images (Stockbyte).

Every effort has been made to contact copyright holders of material reproduced in this book. Any omissions will be rectified in subsequent printings if notice is given to the publishers.

Contents

Shapes

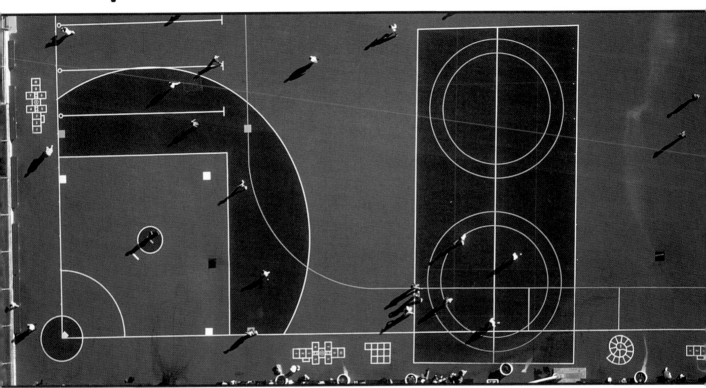

There are shapes all around us.

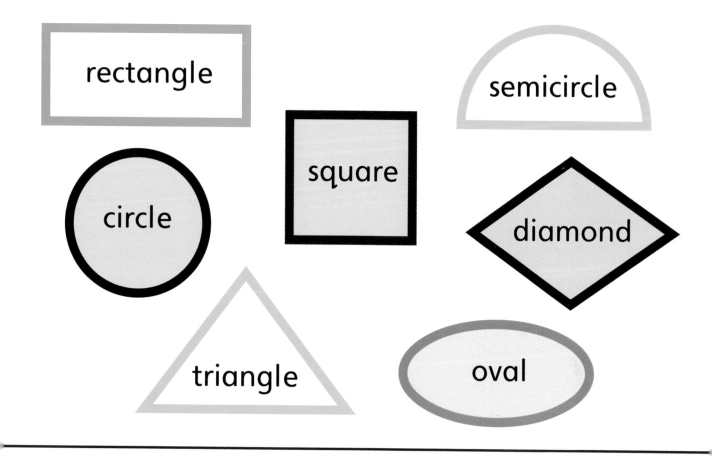

rectangle

semicircle

circle

square

diamond

triangle

oval

Each shape has a name.

Shapes in sport

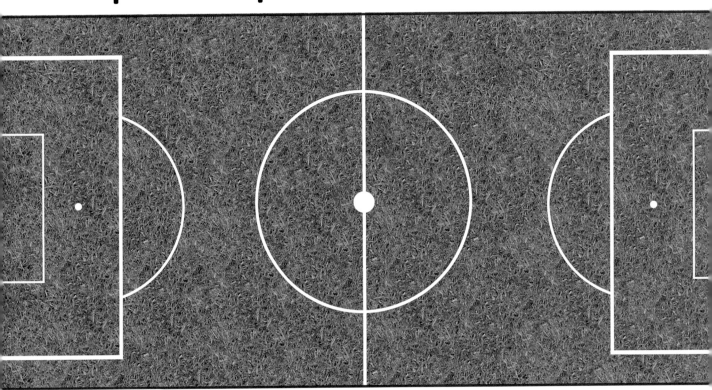

There are many shapes in sport.

What shapes can you see in these flags?

There are squares in these flags.

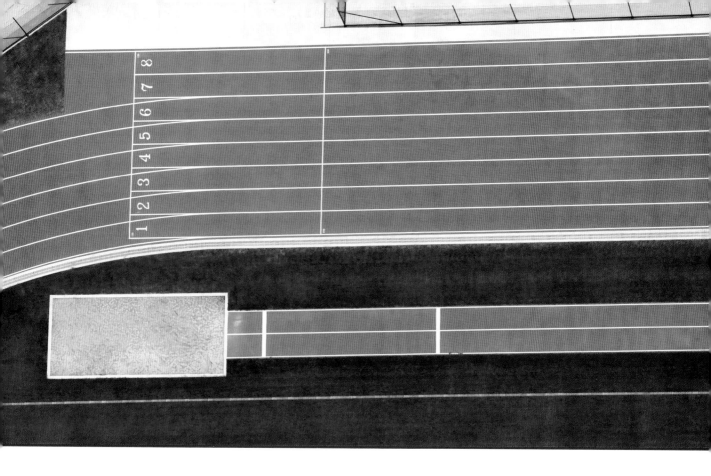

What shape is this sandpit?

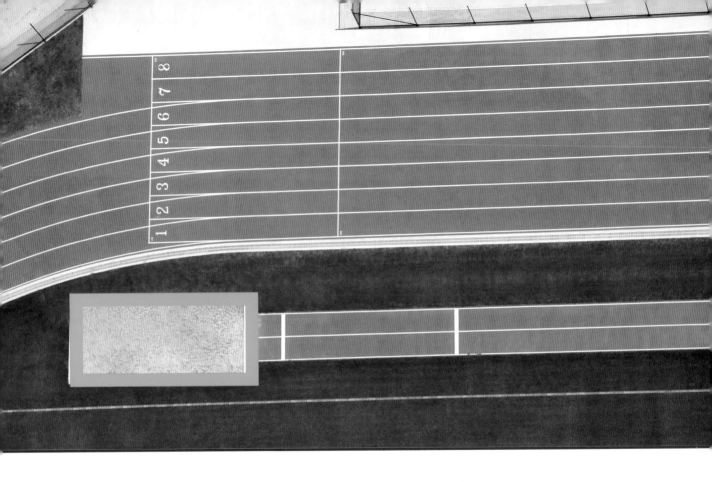

This sandpit is a rectangle.

What shape is this ball?

This ball is an oval.

What shape is this person making?

This person is making a triangle.

What shape is this kayak?

This kayak is a diamond.

What shape is on this ice?

A semicircle is on this ice.

What shape are the wheels on
this bike?

The wheels on this bike are circles.

There are many shapes in sport.
What shapes can you see?

Naming shapes

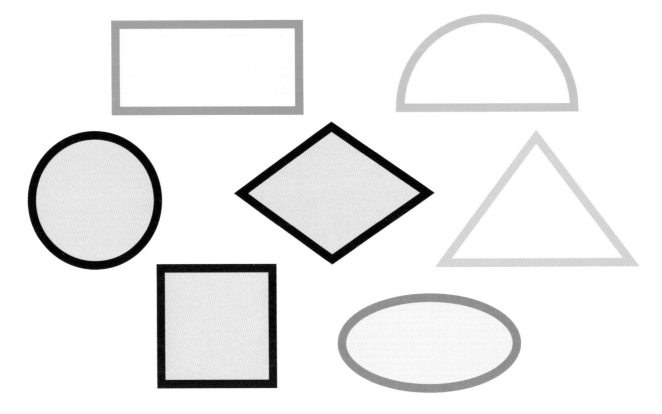

Can you remember the names of these shapes?

Picture glossary

kayak type of boat for one person

Index

Notes for parents and teachers
Before reading
Make two sets of the shapes shown on page 22 out of card. Hold up each shape in turn to the class and ask the children what it is called. Pass each shape round for the children to handle. Shuffle the cards and challenge the children to find the matching cards.

After reading
Shape sort: put out six large hoops in a hall or a garden. In each hoop, place a square bean bag, a ball, and a card triangle. Put the children in two teams. Each team is in charge of three hoops. Challenge each team to end up with each of their hoops having all three items of the same shape before the other team.